MY BLACK ME

MY BLACK ME

A Beginning Book of Black Poetry

Edited by

ARNOLD ADOFF

DUTTON CHILDREN'S BOOKS　　NEW YORK

For My Children
Jaime and Leigh
My Black Me

Library of Congress Cataloging in Publication Data

Adoff, Arnold, comp. My Black me.

SUMMARY: A compilation of poems reflecting thoughts
on being Black by such authors as Langston Hughes,
Lucille Clifton, Nikki Giovanni, and Imamu Amiri Baraka.

1. American poetry—Negro authors. [1. American
poetry—Negro authors. 2. Negroes—Poetry] I. Title.
PS591.N4A29   811'.5'08   73–16445   ISBN 0–525–45216–8

Published in the United States by Dutton Children's Books,
a division of Penguin Books USA Inc.
375 Hudson Street, New York, New York 10014

Designed by Riki Levinson
Printed in the U.S.A.
20 19 18 17 16 15 14 13 12

ACKNOWLEDGMENTS

Copyrighted selections of the following poets are included by permission of the publisher, agent, or poet. This and the following pages constitute an extension of the copyright page. The publisher has made its best efforts to contact all contributors to resecure permissions approval for this 1994 anniversary edition. In such cases where this proved impossible, the original 1974 copyright line and permissions information have been supplied.

IMAMU AMIRI BARAKA (LEROI JONES): "SOS" from *Black Magic*. Copyright © 1969 by LeRoi Jones. Reprinted by permission of The Bobbs-Merrill Company, Inc., and the Ronald Hobbs Literary Agency.

LUCILLE CLIFTON: "Good Times" and "For deLawd" from *Good Times* by Lucille Clifton. Copyright © 1969 by Lucille Clifton. Reprinted by permission of Random House, Inc. "to bobby seale" and "listen children" copyright © 1987 by Lucille Clifton. Reprinted from *Good Woman: Poems and a Memoir 1969–1980*, by Lucille Clifton, by permission of BOA Editions, Ltd.

LLOYD CORBIN, JR. (DJANGATOLUM): "Ali," reprinted by permission of Lloyd Corbin, Jr.

SAM CORNISH: "Death of Dr. King (#1)," "Your Mother," "Montgomery," and "My Brother Is Homemade," from *Generations*, copyright © 1968, 1969, 1970, 1971 by Sam Cornish. Reprinted by permission of Beacon Press. "Cross over the River" and "Sam's World" from *Natural Process*, edited by Ted Wilentz and Tom Weatherly, copyright © 1970 by Hill and Wang, Inc. Reprinted by permission of Hill and Wang, a division of Farrar, Straus & Giroux, Inc.

JACKIE EARLEY: "One Thousand Nine-Hundred & Sixty-Eight Winters . . . ," copyright © 1972 by Jackie Earley, from *Black Spirits*, edited by Woodie King. Reprinted by permission of Random House, Inc.

JAMES EMANUEL: "Old Black Men Say" from *Panther Man*, copyright © 1970 by James Emanuel. Reprinted by permission of Broadside Press.

JULIA FIELDS: "Aardvark" from *Nine Black Poets*, copyright © 1993 by Julia Fields. Reprinted by permission of Julia Fields.

This Book of Black

This book of Black is for you. Black poems for Black sisters and brothers. Black poems for *all* sisters and brothers. Of every race. Every open face. Poems that help you know your inside faces. Your human pieces put together strong and fine. Human poems.

It is a book of Black poetry. Poems by Black American poets of our time. Poems that are old and young and in between. Poems that tell about being Black. Poems that tell about being.

And this is a *beginning* book of Black. There have been hundreds of Black men and women, slave and free, who have been poets. Are poets today. Are becoming poets for tomorrow. Their poems are shouts and songs. Cries and laughs. Facts and fantasy. Pictures and words. Good strong poems of love and hate and all the rest that's in between.

Some of those poems are in this book. Many more are in other books. Read this book. Go out to other books. Come back to this one. Go out again. Keep on going. Write your own poems. Keep on.

Let all these poems help you feel strong inside. Let all these poems push you out of your chair to stand tall. Then sit back down again and think about what you are right now. About what you can become tomorrow.

This book of Black is for you. Young brothers and sisters of every race. In every big city and small town place. All power to you. Use these poems for power and love. Like cornbread and kisses. Words and music will make you strong. Stay strong for yourself. Strong for the people. Read on.

This twentieth anniversary arrives at a time of struggle and change. Poets and teachers, librarians and parents, are working harder than ever to show the true faces of a multicultural nation. All of you deserve this spotlight on our truths: our chance, again, to light up all the dark corners. We must work hard to present the varied voices of our people, to all our children. We need to sing and shout, in love and anger. We need to call attention to rich histories, progress and problems of our present, the possibilities of our woven-together futures on this spinning rock.

Power to the poets. Peace on us all.

Arnold Adoff
Yellow Springs, Ohio
1994

Contents

I

Listen Children
LUCILLE CLIFTON

listen children
keep this in the place
you have for keeping
always
keep it all ways

we have never hated black

listen
we have been ashamed
hopeless   tired   mad
but always
all ways
we loved us

we have always loved each other
children   all ways

pass it on

Our Black People
KALI GROSVENOR

Our Black
People are
your and my
People We Know
they can love
let this be true
For Me and All
of you.

It's a New Kind of Day
KALI GROSVENOR

It's a New Kind of Day
It's a New Kind of Day
It's the love that make
a New kind of day

It's a New Kind
of D. It's a New kind
of day. It's a New
kind. love. help us with
this love. lord we love
to much.

The Real People Loves One Another

ROB PENNY

the real people loves one another
the rest bees shaming, bees walkin
backwards under the sun.

My People

LANGSTON HUGHES

The night is beautiful,
So the faces of my people.

The stars are beautiful,
So the eyes of my people.

Beautiful, also, is the sun.
Beautiful, also, are the souls of my people.

Sun Song
LANGSTON HUGHES

Sun and softness,
Sun and the beaten hardness of the earth,
Sun and the song of all the sun-stars
Gathered together—
Dark ones of Africa,
I bring you my songs
To sing on the Georgia roads.

From African Poems

DON L. LEE

WE'RE an Africanpeople
hard-softness burning black.
the earth's magic color our veins.
an Africanpeople are we;
burning blacker softly, softer.

Awareness
DON L. LEE

BLACK   PEOPLE   THINK

PEOPLE   BLACK   PEOPLE

THINK   PEOPLE   THINK

BLACK   PEOPLE   THINK—

THINK   BLACK.

Black People
TED JOANS

I SEE BLACK PEOPLE
I HEAR BLACK PEOPLE
I SMELL BLACK PEOPLE
I TASTE BLACK PEOPLE
I TOUCH BLACK PEOPLE
BLACK PEOPLE IS MY MOMMA
BLACK PEOPLE IS MY DAD
BLACK PEOPLE IS   MY SISTER,BROTHER,UNCLE,AUNT,
     AND COUSINS
BLACK PEOPLE IS   ALL WE   BLACK PEOPLE   EVER HAD
NOW THAT WE THE BLACK PEOPLE KNOW THAT
WE THE BLACK PEOPLE SHOULD BE GLAD

II

To P. J. (2 yrs old who sed write a poem for me in Portland, Oregon)

SONIA SANCHEZ

if i cud ever write a
poem as beautiful as u
little 2/yr/old/brotha,
i wud laugh, jump, leap
up and touch the stars
cuz u be the poem i try for
each time i pick up a pen and paper.
u. and Morani and Mungu
be our blue/blk/stars that
will shine on our lives and
makes us finally BE.
if i cud ever write a poem as beautiful
as u, little 2/yr/old/brotha,
poetry wud go out of bizness.

From **Riot Rimes U.S.A.** #78

RAY PATTERSON

I just once want to feel
America is proud of me—black.
I just want America
To get off my back.

From **Riot Rimes U.S.A.** #79

RAY PATTERSON

You got to be scared
Both ways
To know what I mean,
And be where I've been—
Scared beating on the door
From the outside,
And scared when they let you in.

Good Morning
LANGSTON HUGHES

Good morning, daddy!
I was born here, he said,
watched Harlem grow
until colored folks spread
from river to river
across the middle of Manhattan
out of Penn Station
dark tenth of a nation,
planes from Puerto Rico,
and holds of boats, chico,
up from Cuba Haiti Jamaica,
in buses marked New York
from Georgia Florida Louisiana
to Harlem Brooklyn the Bronx
but most of all to Harlem
dusky sash across Manhattan

I've seen them come dark
   wondering
   wide-eyed
   dreaming
out of Penn Station—
but the trains are late.
The gates open—
but there're bars
at each gate.

   What happens
   to a dream deferred?

Daddy, ain't you heard?

Dream Deferred
LANGSTON HUGHES

What happens to a dream deferred?

Does it dry up
like a raisin in the sun?
Or fester like a sore—
And then run?
Does it stink like rotten meat?
Or crust and sugar over—
like a syrupy sweet?

Maybe it just sags
like a heavy load.

Or does it explode?

I Was Jus

BOB O'MEALLY

i was jus
anovah one
uh-duh chiren
(which we all was all jus chirens)

an we all
set hunched-up at
pop-top desses all
in rows wit chalk lines
drew on   duh flo

i usta put my head down
on duh dess my
hans on   duh bottom
uh-duh pop-top dess an

stop tappinG your foot younG man
wheredoyouthinkyouare
in the JUNGLE!?!
no ma'm
an i'd cross mah legs an
i'd drum out a hellfire   protess
in secret.

It Aint No

BOB O'MEALLY

it aint no
bookstos
in de Berry
where i lives

teacher say read
mama say read granma say
read evythin you get yo
hans on boy
but
it just aint no bookstos
in de Berry
where i lives

lady in   de liberry
say she aint got
no books on black folks
uncle jake (he wento collige)
he say read books on blacks
say evythin else aint bout me
lady she say try de booksto
guess uncle jake dont know
guess lady dont know neivah

aint no bookstos
here aint no
bookstos where i lives
in de Berry

Ten Years Old

NIKKI GIOVANNI

i paid my 30¢ and rode by the bus
window all the way down

i felt a little funny with no hair
on my head
but my knees were shiny 'cause
aunty mai belle cleaned me up
and i got off on time and walked
past the lions and the guard straight
up to the desk and said
   "dr. doo little steroscope please"
and this really old woman said
   "Do You Have A Library Card?"
and i said
   "i live here up the street"

and she said
   "Do You Have a LIBRARY Card?"
and i said
   "this is the only place i can use
      the steroscope for
   dr. dooolittle miss washington
      brought us here this spring
   to see it"
and another lady said
   "GIVE THE BOY WHAT HE WANT.
    HE WANT TO LEAD THE RACE"
and i said
   "no ma'am i want to see dr. dooolittle"
and she said "same thang son same thang"

Poem for Flora
NIKKI GIOVANNI

when she was little
and colored and ugly with short
straightened hair
and a very pretty smile
she went to sunday school to hear
'bout nebuchadnezzar the king
of the jews

and she would listen

shadrach, meshach and abednego in the fire

and she would learn

how god was neither north
nor south east or west
with no color but all
she remembered was that
Sheba was Black and comely

and she would think

i want to be
like that

Winter Poem
NIKKI GIOVANNI

once a snowflake fell
on my brow and i loved
it so much and i kissed
it and it was happy and called its cousins
and brothers and a web
of snow engulfed me then
i reached to love them all
and i squeezed them and they became
a spring rain and i stood perfectly
still and was a flower

III

August 8
NORMAN JORDAN

There is no break

between

yesterday and today

mother and son

air and earth

all are a part

of the other

like

with this typewriter

I am connected

with these words

and these words

with this paper

and this paper with you.

From **Blackwoman Poems**
DON L. LEE

soft: the way her eyes view her children.
hard: her hands; a comment on her will.
warm: just the way she is, jim!
sure: as yesterday, she's tomorrow's tomorrow.

Sam's World

SAM CORNISH

sam's mother has
grey combed hair

she will never touch
it with a hot iron

she leaves it
the way the lord
intended

she wears it proudly
a black and grey
round head of hair

Your Mother

SAM CORNISH

your mother
in the market
place searches
for fish
pinches oranges
watches prices
change for
the weekend
she checks the dirt
under the butcher's
fingernail her feet
slip in water
and fish scales
hamburger looks
dead behind dirty
counter glass
flies
even in the winter
live here

For deLawd
LUCILLE CLIFTON

people say they have a hard time
understanding how I
go on about my business
playing my Ray Charles
hollering at the kids—
seem like my Afro
cut off in some old image
would show I got a long memory
and I come from a line
of black and going on women
who got used to making it through murdered sons
and who grief kept on pushing
who fried chicken
ironed
swept off the back steps
who grief kept
for their still alive sons
for their sons coming
for their sons gone
just pushing

Portrait
CAROLYN RODGERS

mama spent pennies
in uh gallon milk jug
saved pennies
fuh four babies
college educashun

and when the babies
got bigger they would
secretly "borrow" mama's
pennies to buy candy

and pop cause mama
saved extras
fuh college educashuns
and pop and candy

was uh non-credit in bad teeth
mama pooled pennies
in uh gallon milk jug,
Borden's by the way

and the babies went
to school cause mama saved
and spent and paid
fuh four babies

college educashuns
mama spent pennies
                          and nickels
                          and quarters
                          and dollars

and one life.
mama spent her life
in uh gallon milk jug
fuh four black babies
college educashuns.

Good Times
LUCILLE CLIFTON

My Daddy has paid the rent
and the insurance man is gone
and the lights is back on
and my uncle Brud has hit
for one dollar straight
and they is good times
good times
good times

My Mama has made bread
and Grampaw has come
and everybody is drunk
and dancing in the kitchen
and singing in the kitchen
oh these is good times
good times
good times

oh children think about the
good times

My Brother Is Homemade

SAM CORNISH

my brother is homemade
like he was the first real
black boy i ever knew

before Richard Wright
or James Baldwin found
black summers
he taught me how to drink at age
five and a half

& cleaned the streets
with bullies and stolen
bread and ice cream

he came into this
color thing lighter
than me
& to prove a point
grew darker
than most

Monument in Black

VANESSA HOWARD

Put my Black father on the penny
let him smile at me on the silver dime
put my mother on the dollar
for they've suffered for more than
three eternities of time
and all money can't repay.

Make a monument of my grandfather
let him stand in Washington
for he's suffered more than
three light years
standing idle in the dark
hero of wars that weren't begun.

Name a holiday for my brother
on a sunny day peaceful and warm
for he's fighting for freedom he
won't be granted
all my Black brothers in Vietnam
resting idle in unkept graves.

IV

Glory, Glory. . .

RAY PATTERSON

Across Grandmother's knees
A kindly sun
Laid a yellow quilt.

Knoxville, Tennessee

NIKKI GIOVANNI

I always like summer
best
you can eat fresh corn
from daddy's garden
and okra
and greens
and cabbage
and lots of
barbecue
and buttermilk
and homemade ice-cream
at the church picnic

and listen to
gospel music
outside
at the church
homecoming
and go to the mountains with
your grandmother
and go barefooted
and be warm
all the time
not only when you go to bed
and sleep

#4

DOUGHTRY LONG

Where my grandmother lived
there was always sweet potato pie
and thirds on green beans and
songs and words of how we'd
survived it all.
Blackness.
And the wind
a soft lull
in the pecan tree
whispered
Ethiopia
    Ethiopia, Ethiopia
E-th-io-piaaaaa!

A Grandfather Poem

WILLIAM J. HARRIS

A grandfather poem
must use words of great dignity.

It can not
contain words like:
Ubangi
rolling pin
popsicle,

but words like:
Supreme Court
graceful
wise.

Old Black Men Say

JAMES EMANUEL

They say "Son"
(always start with son)
"watch out, cause them folks
is MEAN
when you rile em"—
as if I cant be mean
(grandaddy walked like
old Black men,
bent over where they hit im
ridin drinkin cussin laughin
throwed their bottle on his street
the sheriff didnt do a thing),

yeah they say "Listen. I KNOW"
(daddy didnt listen
didnt know, mamma never
told how he died)
and they squint and chew on how I feel
hearin that old jive
bout what they KNOW
(they know they took that crap
they died

they dead right now
xcep for me
not listenin).

"Boy you aint listenin"
(but somethin in they voice
say go head
say if you strong enough
go be a fool,
somethin turns me loose
stays at the door
like fist on that old walkin cane
they didnt need,
took just to poke they minds
around the ground).

When I leave
them old men's noses
suck in like they painin smart,
spittin sideways
lookin me up and down
like a crop they raised.

Im gonna rile them folks
like I been riled,
gonna be a fool
maybe,
whatever they raised—
them old Black men.

I've Got a Home in That Rock...

RAY PATTERSON

I had an uncle, once, who kept a rock in his pocket—
Always did, up to the day he died.
And as far as I know, that rock is still with him,
Holding down some dust of his thighbone.

From Mississippi he'd got that rock, he'd say—
Or, sometimes, from Tennessee: a different place
    each year
He told it, how he'd snatched it up when he first
    left home—
Running, he'd say—to remind him, when times
    got hard
Enough to make him homesick, what home was
    really like.

V

Cross over the River

SAM CORNISH

harriet tubman
coming down the river
black face
reflected in the water

harriet tubman
in a gunboat
singing

slaves on the shore
singing
there is a home   somewhere

Montgomery
SAM CORNISH

FOR ROSA PARKS

white woman have you heard
she is too tired to sit in the back
her feet two hundred years old

move to the back or walk
around to the side door how
long can a woman be a cow

your feet will not move
and you never listen
but even if it rains empty

seats will ride through town
i walk for my children
my feet two hundred years old

Ali

LLOYD CORBIN, JR.
(DJANGATOLUM)

Ali
Is our prince
Regal and Black
A glass that could fall
but never break
A flower without rain
that never could die
Ali
Is our prince

To Bobby Seale
LUCILLE CLIFTON

feel free.
like my daddy
always said
jail wasn't made
for dogs,
was made for
men

To Malcolm X
JULIUS THOMPSON

he knew someone
would take his
life. he lived
never fearing
when the end
would come.
he was a true
brother. he
realized before
the Time
that all men
are men
and children
of each other.
this was his
greatness,
to bring to us
that all men
are really brothers.

I Remember. . .

MAE JACKSON

i remember. . .
january,
1968
it's snow,
the desire that i had to build
a black snowman
and place him upon
Malcolm's grave.

Aardvark

JULIA FIELDS

Since
    Malcolm died
    That old aardvark
    has got a sort of fame
    for himself—
    I mean, of late, when I read
    The dictionary the first
    Thing I see
    Is that animal staring at me.
And then
    I think of Malcolm—
    How he read
    in the prisons
    And on the planes
    And everywhere
    And how he wrote
    About old Aardvark.
Looks like Malcolm X helped
Bring attention to a lot of things
We never thought about before.

Death of Dr. King #1

SAM CORNISH

we sit outside
the bars   the dime stores
everything is closed today

we are mourning
our hands filled with bricks
a brother is dead

my eyes are white and cold
water is in my hands

this is grief

VI

Dream Variation

LANGSTON HUGHES

To fling my arms wide
In some place of the sun,
To whirl and to dance
Till the white day is done.
Then rest at cool evening
Beneath a tall tree
While night comes on gently,
    Dark like me—
That is my dream!

To fling my arms wide
In the face of the sun,
Dance! Whirl! Whirl!
Till the quick day is done.
Rest at pale evening. . .
A tall, slim tree. . .
Night coming tenderly
    Black like me.

Final Curve

LANGSTON HUGHES

When you turn the corner
And you run into *yourself*
Then you know that you have turned
All the corners that are left.

Black Is Best

LARRY THOMPSON

Black is best.
         My mother forgot to tell me.
But I told her
        that black is best.
      And she says: Boy hush your mouth
I again say:
        Black is best mamma.
        And she hit me.
    But I keep saying:
          Black is best.

One Thousand Nine-Hundred & Sixty-Eight Winters. . .

JACKIE EARLEY

Got up this morning
Feeling good & Black
Thinking black thoughts
Did black things
Played all my black records
And minded my own black bidness!

Put on my best black clothes
Walked out my black door
And. . .

Lord have Mercy!
White
Snow!

Were Is My Head Going

KALI GROSVENOR

Were is my head Going
Were is my head Going
up Down arond Sidways
Black White turning
Were is it Goning
its Going Black
thats were

What Color Is Black?

BARBARA MAHONE

black is the color of
my little brother's mind
the grey streaks
in my mother's hair
black is the color of
my yellow cousin's smile
the scars upon my
neighbor's wrinkled face.
the color of
the blood we lose
the color of our eyes
is black.
our love of self
of others
brothers sisters
people of a thousand
shades of black
all one.
black is the color of
the feeling that we share
the love we must express
the color of our strength
is black.

Do Not Think

CAROL FREEMAN

Do not think
We
Want to harm you
if
We touch
Your
Confused mind
And
Pull you into
Blackness
—we only want to bring you home.

SOS

IMAMU AMIRI BARAKA
(LEROI JONES)

Calling black people
Calling all black people, man woman child
Wherever you are, calling you, urgent, come in
Black People, come in, wherever you are, urgent,
calling you, calling all black people
calling all black people, come in, black people,
come on in.

The Poets

IMAMU AMIRI BARAKA (LEROI JONES) was born in Newark, New Jersey, in 1934. He is one of the most important American writers of our time. Some of his books of poetry include *Black Magic (Collected Poetry: 1961–1967)* and *Spirit, Reach*. He is the author of *Dutchman, The Slave,* and other plays which have been produced in New York and around the world. A visiting professor at Rutgers University since 1988, he is also the author of *Blues People: Negro Music in White America* and *The Music: Reflections on Jazz and Blues.*

LUCILLE CLIFTON was born in Depew, New York, in 1936. Her books of poetry include *Good Woman: Poems and a Memoir 1969–1980* and *Good News About the Earth*. Some of her books for children are *Some of the Days of Everett Anderson, The Black B C's, Everett Anderson's Christmas Coming,* and *The Boy Who Didn't Believe in Spring.*

LLOYD CORBIN, JR. (DJANGATOLUM) was born in New York City in 1949. His poems have appeared in many anthologies, including *The Me Nobody Knows, Black Out Loud,* and *The Poetry of Black America.*

SAM CORNISH was born in Baltimore, Maryland, in 1935. He is the author of *Your Hand in Mine, Generations, Nineteen Thirty-Five: A Memoir,* and *Folks Like Me,* among other books.

JACKIE EARLEY was born in Buffalo, New York, in 1939, and raised in Ohio. Her poetry has appeared in many collections, including *We Speak As Liberators: Young Black Poets* and *Black Spirits*.

JAMES EMANUEL was born in Nebraska in 1921. His books of poems include *The Treehouse and Other Poems*, *Panther Man*, *Whole Grain: Collected Poems*, and *A Poet's Mind*, among others. He now lives in France.

JULIA FIELDS was born in Uniontown, Alabama, in 1938, and now lives in Washington, D.C. Her poetry has appeared in many anthologies, including *New Negro Poets: USA*, *The Poetry of the Negro*, and *The Poetry of Black America*. A collection of her poetry, *East of Moonlight*, was published in 1973. She is also the author of *The Green Lion of Zion Street*, a book for children.

CAROL FREEMAN was born in Rayville, Louisiana, in 1942. Her poetry has appeared in such anthologies as *Black Fire*, *The Poetry of the Negro*, and *The Poetry of Black America*.

NIKKI GIOVANNI was born in Knoxville, Tennessee, in 1943, and grew up in Cincinnati, Ohio. She is now a professor at Virginia Polytechnic Institute and State University at Blacksburg. Her books of poetry include *Black Feeling, Black Talk, Black Judgement*; *Re-Creation*; *Sacred Cows . . . and Other Edibles*; and *My House*. Her books for children include *Spin a Soft Black Song* and *Ego-Tripping and Other Poems for Young People*.

KALI GROSVENOR was six and seven when she wrote the poems in *Poems by Kali*. She was eight when this first book of hers was published. Today she lives in Washington, D.C.

She is the executive director of the Phillipps-Murray Foundation, works in film production, and writes songs. She also reads poetry to her two-year-old daughter, Charlotte Rose.

WILLIAM J. HARRIS was born in Yellow Springs, Ohio, in 1942. His poetry has been published in many anthologies, including *Nine Black Poets*, *Black Out Loud*, *Natural Process*, and *The Poetry of Black America*. He is also the author of *The Poetry and Poetics of Amiri Baraka: The Jazz Aesthetic*.

VANESSA HOWARD was born in Brooklyn, New York, in 1955. She is the author of *A Screaming Whisper*, and her poems have appeared in such anthologies as *The Voice of the Children* and *Soulscript*.

LANGSTON HUGHES was born in Joplin, Missouri, in 1902. During his long career he was one of the most important poets of Black America. Some of his books of poetry are *The Weary Blues*, *The Dream Keeper*, *Montage of a Dream Deferred*, *Selected Poems*, *Ask Your Mama*, and *The Panther and the Lash*. He wrote many novels, stories, and plays, and edited two important anthologies of Black American poetry, *The Poetry of the Negro* and *New Negro Poets: USA*.

MAE JACKSON was born in Earl, Arkansas, in 1946. Her poems have been published in many anthologies, including *Black Out Loud*, *Black Spirits*, and *The Poetry of Black America*. A collection of her poems, *Can I Poet with You*, appeared in 1969.

TED JOANS was born in Cairo, Illinois, in 1928. He is a painter and jazz musician as well as a poet. His books of poetry include *Black Pow-Wow* and *Afrodisia*.

NORMAN JORDAN was born in Ansted, West Virginia, in 1938. His poetry has been included in many anthologies, including *The New Black Poetry, Black Out Loud, The Poetry of the Negro, Black Spirits,* and *The Poetry of Black America.* His books of poetry are *Destination: Ashes* and *Above Maya.*

DON L. LEE (HAKI MADHUBUTI) was born in Little Rock, Arkansas, in 1942. His books of poetry include *Think Black!; Black Pride; Don't Cry, Scream; We Walk the Way of the New World;* and *Directionscore: Selected and New Poems.* Mr. Madhubuti is publisher of Third World Press.

DOUGHTRY LONG was born in Atlanta, Georgia, in 1942. His work has appeared in many anthologies, and his books of poetry include *Black Love, Black Hope* and *Song for Nia.*

BARBARA MAHONE was born in Chicago, Illinois, in 1944. Her poetry has appeared in many anthologies, and a collection of her work, *Sugarfields,* was published in 1970.

BOB O'MEALLY was born in Washington, D.C., in 1948. He is the author of *Lady Day: The Many Faces of Billie Holiday* and the editor of *New Essays on "Invisible Man."* In the poem "It Aint No," the "Berry" is Roxbury, the Black community of Boston, Massachusetts. He now is a Zora Neale Hurston professor of English at Columbia University.

RAY PATTERSON was born in New York City in 1929. His poetry has been published in most of the major anthologies of Black poetry, including *The Poetry of the Negro* and *The Poetry of Black America.* He is also the author of *26 Ways of Looking at a Black Man* and *Romance, Rhythm, and Revolution: New and Selected Poetry.*

ROB PENNY was born in Opelika, Alabama, in 1940. He is an instructor at the University of Pittsburgh, writes plays, and helps to publish Black writers in the Pittsburgh area. A collection of his poetry, *Black Tones of Truth*, appeared in 1970.

CAROLYN RODGERS was born and raised in Chicago, Illinois. Her poetry has appeared in such anthologies as *Natural Process*, *We Speak As Liberators*, and *The Poetry of Black America*. Her books of poetry include *Paper Soul*, *Songs of a Blackbird*, *2 Love Raps*, a broadside, and *Blues Gittin Up*.

SONIA SANCHEZ was born in Birmingham, Alabama, in 1935. Her work has been included in many collections, including *Natural Process*, *The Black Poets*, *New Black Voices*, and *The Poetry of Black America*. Ms. Sanchez is one of the most influential poets to come out of the 1960's. Her books include *Homecoming*, *We a Baddddd People*, *It's a New Day: Poems for Young Brothas and Sistuhs*, *Three Hundred and Sixty Degrees of Blackness Comin at You*, *Homegirls and Handgrenades*, *I've Been a Woman*, and *Under a Soprano Sky*. She is now a professor of English at Temple University.

JULIUS THOMPSON was born in Vicksburg, Mississippi. His poetry has appeared in many publications, and a collection of his poems, *Hopes Tied Up in Promises*, was issued in 1970. He is also the author of *The Black Press in Mississippi: 1865–1985*.

LARRY THOMPSON was born in Seneca, South Carolina, in 1950. His poems have appeared in such anthologies as *Black Out Loud*, *It Is the Poem Singing into Your Eyes: Anthology of New Young Poets*, and *The Poetry of Black America*.

Index to Authors

Index to First Lines

Born and raised in New York City, ARNOLD ADOFF was a teacher and counselor in the New York public schools for twelve years. He studied American history and literature at the City College of New York and at Columbia University, and he studied writing at the New School in New York City. His more than thirty books for young people and their "older allies" since 1968 include such noted anthologies as *I Am the Darker Brother* and *The Poetry of Black America*. Volumes of his own poetry and "poet's prose" include *Black Is Brown Is Tan*, *All the Colors of the Race*, and *In for Winter, Out for Spring*. He received the NCTE (National Council of Teachers of English) Award for Excellence in Poetry for Children for the body of his work.

Mr. Adoff and his wife, esteemed author Virginia Hamilton, now divide their time between Yellow Springs, Ohio, and New York City. They have two grown children, Leigh Hamilton and Jaime Levi. Mr. Adoff still enjoys traveling around the country to teach, read his poems, and work with young readers and writers in their schools.